# My New Glasses

by Kate Sternberg

illustrated by Toni Goffe

HOUGHTON MIFFLIN COMPANY BOSTON

Atlanta   Dallas   Geneva, Illinois   Palo Alto   Princeton   Toronto

With my new glasses,
I can see

Something on the table —
Something special for me!

With my new glasses,
I can see

My brother in the chair,
And something on the table —
Something special for me!

With my new glasses,
I can see

The dog in the basket,
My brother in the chair,
And something on the table —
Something special for me!

With my new glasses,
I can see

The cat in the window,
The dog in the basket,
My brother in the chair,
And something on the table —
Something special for me!

With my new glasses,
I can see

My mother in the garden,
The cat in the window,
The dog in the basket,
My brother in the chair,
And something on the table —
Something special for me!

With my new glasses,
I can see

My father at the door,
My mother in the garden,
The cat in the window,
The dog in the basket,
My brother in the chair,
And something on the table —
Something special for me!

With my new glasses,
I can see

A bee flying in the air,
My father at the door,
My mother in the garden,
The cat in the window,
The dog in the basket,
My brother in the chair,
And something on the table —
Something special for me!

With my new glasses,
I can see

A bee out the window,
My father on the table,
My mother at the door,
The cat in the garden,
The dog in the chair,
My brother in the basket,
And something flying in the air —
Something special for me!

WOW!